The Three Bears & 15 Other Stories

The Three Bears

&

15 other stories

selected and illustrated

by Anne Rockwell

A Harper Trophy Book

THOMAS Y. CROWELL   NEW YORK

The Three Bears & 15 Other Stories
Copyright © 1975 by Anne Rockwell
For information address
Harper & Row Junior Books, 10 East 53rd Street,
New York, N.Y. 10022. Published simultaneously in
Canada by Fitzhenry & Whiteside Limited, Toronto.
Designed by Anne Rockwell
First Harper Trophy edition, 1984.

Library of Congress Cataloging in Publication Data
Rockwell, Anne F.
    The three bears and fifteen other stories, selected
and illustrated by Anne Rockwell.

    Summary: Sixteen famous children's stories including
"Lazy Jack," "Three Little Pigs," "The Gingerbread Man,"
and "The Shoemaker and the Elves."
    [1. Folklore.   2. Fairy tales.]   I. Title.
PZ8.1.R6Th   398.2   74-5381
ISBN 0-690-00597-0
ISBN 0-690-00598-9 (lib. bdg.)
ISBN 0-06-440142-1 (pbk.)

for Hannah,
Elizabeth & Oliver

Contents

THE THREE BEARS

Once upon a time there were three bears who lived together in a house of their own in a wood. One of them was a little wee bear, and one was a middle-sized bear, and the third was a great big bear. They each had a bowl for their porridge—a little bowl for the little wee bear, and a middle-sized bowl for the middle-sized bear, and a great big bowl for the great big bear. And they each had a chair to sit on— a little chair for the little wee bear, and a middle-sized chair for the middle-sized bear, and a great big chair for the great big bear. And they each had

1

a bed to sleep in—a little bed for the little wee bear,
and a middle-sized bed for the middle-sized bear,
and a great big bed for the great big bear.

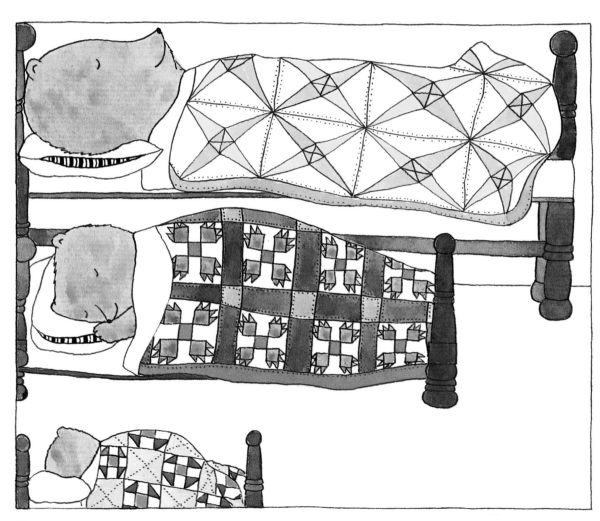

One day, after they had made the porridge for
their breakfast and poured it into their bowls, they
walked out in the woods while the porridge was
cooling. A little girl named Goldilocks passed by the
house and looked in at the window. And then she
looked in at the keyhole, and when she saw that there
was no one home, she lifted the latch on the door.

The door was not locked because the bears were good bears who never did anyone any harm and never thought that anyone would harm them. So Goldilocks opened the door and walked in. She was very glad to see the porridge on the table, as she was hungry from walking in the woods, and so she set about helping herself.

First she tasted the porridge of the great big bear, but that was too hot for her. Next she tasted the porridge of the middle-sized bear, but that was too cold for her. And then she tasted the porridge of the little wee bear, and that was neither too hot nor too cold but just right, and she liked it so much that she ate it all up.

Then Goldilocks sat down on the chair of the great big bear, but that was too hard for her. And

then she sat down on the chair of the middle-sized bear, and that was too soft for her. And then she

sat down on the chair of the little wee bear, and that was neither too hard nor too soft, but just right. So she seated herself in it, and there she sat until she sat the bottom out of the chair and down she came upon the floor.

Then Goldilocks went upstairs to the bedroom where the three bears slept. And first she lay down upon the bed of the great big bear, but that was too high for her. And next she lay down upon the bed of the middle-sized bear, but that was too low for her. But when she lay down upon the bed of the little wee bear, it was neither too high nor too low, but just right. So she covered herself up comfortably and fell fast asleep.

When the three bears thought their porridge would be cool enough for them to eat, they came home for breakfast. Now Goldilocks had left the spoon of the great big bear standing in the porridge.

"Somebody has been eating my porridge!" said the great big bear in a great, rough gruff voice.

Then the middle-sized bear looked at its porridge and saw the spoon was standing in it, too.

"Somebody has been eating my porridge!" said the middle-sized bear in a middle-sized voice.

Then the little wee bear looked at its bowl, and there was the spoon standing in the bowl, but the porridge was all gone.

"Somebody has been eating my porridge and has eaten it all up!" said the little wee bear in a little wee voice.

Upon this, the three bears, seeing that someone had come into their house and eaten up all the little wee bear's breakfast, began to look around them. Now Goldilocks had not put the cushion straight when she rose from the chair of the great big bear.

"Somebody has been sitting in my chair!" said the great big bear in a great, rough gruff voice.

And Goldilocks had squashed down the soft cushion of the middle-sized bear.

"Somebody has been sitting in my chair!" said the middle-sized bear in a middle-sized voice.

"Somebody has been sitting in my chair, and has sat the bottom through!" said the little wee bear in a little wee voice.

Then the three bears thought that they had better look farther in case it was a burglar, so they went upstairs into their bedroom. Now Goldilocks had pulled the pillow of the great big bear out of its place.

"Somebody has been lying in my bed!" said the great big bear in a great, rough gruff voice.

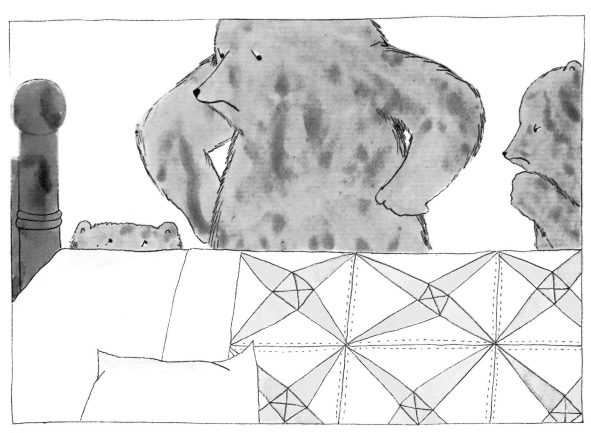

And Goldilocks had pulled the cover of the middle-sized bear out of its place.

"Somebody has been lying in my bed!" said the middle-sized bear in a middle-sized voice.

But when the little wee bear came to look at its bed, there was the pillow in its place. But upon the pillow? There was Goldilocks' head, which was not in its place, for she had no business there.

"Somebody has been lying in my bed, and here she is still," said the little wee bear in a little wee voice.

11

Now Goldilocks had heard in her sleep the great, rough gruff voice of the great big bear, but she was so fast asleep that it was no more to her than the rumbling of distant thunder. And she had heard the middle-sized voice of the middle-sized bear, but it was only as if she had heard someone speaking in a dream. But when she heard the little wee voice of the little wee bear, it was so sharp and so shrill that it woke her up at once.

Up she sat, and when she saw the three bears on one side of the bed, she tumbled out at the other and ran to the window. Now the window was open, for the bears were good, tidy bears who always opened their bedroom window in the morning to let in the fresh air and sunshine. So Goldilocks jumped out through the window and ran away, and the three bears never saw anything more of her.

THE LION and THE MOUSE

A lion lay sleeping. A little mouse ran across his paw. That tickled the lion and woke him up. He roared and grabbed the little mouse.

"Please," said the little mouse, "do not hurt me. I am sorry I woke you up, but if you do not hurt me, I promise I will do something good for you someday."

The lion laughed. "How silly," he thought. "What could a tiny little mouse do for a big, strong lion like me?" But he let him go.

Soon after, the lion was walking through the forest when suddenly he was caught in a net some hunters had made to trap him. He roared and roared, and his roars made the leaves on the trees tremble, but still he could not free himself from the net.

Far away the little mouse heard him roar. He hurried to the place where the big lion lay trapped.

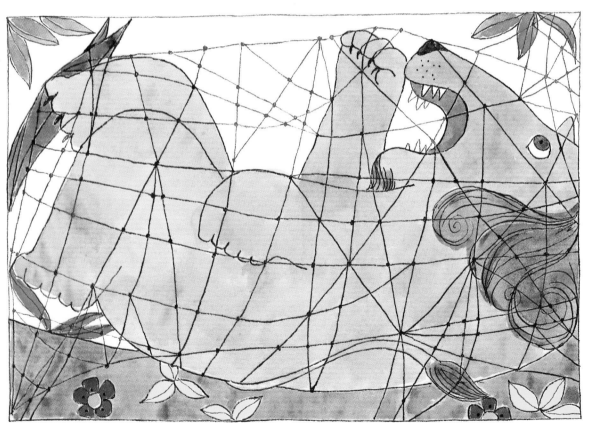

"Remember, I promised you I would someday do something good for you," said the little mouse, and he began to nibble on the ropes of the net with his sharp little teeth. He nibbled and nibbled and nibbled some more until there was a big hole in the net.

Then the lion was free, and the lion and the mouse walked away together.

THE COCK AND THE MOUSE AND THE LITTLE RED HEN

Once upon a time there was a hill, and on the hill there was a pretty little house. It had one little green door and four little windows, and in this house there lived a cock and a mouse and a little red hen. On another hill, across the valley, there was another little house. It was very ugly. It had a door that wouldn't shut and two broken windows, and all the paint was peeling off. And in this house there lived a big bad fox and four bad little foxes.

One morning these four bad little foxes came to the big bad fox and said, "Oh, Father, we are so hungry!"

"We had nothing to eat yesterday," said one.

"And not much the day before," said another.

The big bad fox shook his head, for he was thinking. At last he said in a big gruff voice, "On the hill over there I see a house. And in that house there lives a cock."

"And a mouse," screamed two of the little foxes.

"And a little red hen!" screamed the other two.

"And they are nice and fat," said the big bad fox. "This very day I'll take my sack, and I will go down this hill, across the stream, up that hill, and in at that door, and into my sack I will put the cock and the mouse and the little red hen."

So the four little foxes jumped for joy, and the big bad fox took his sack and went on his way.

Now that morning the cock and the mouse had both gotten out of the wrong side of bed. The cock said the day was too hot, and the mouse said the day was too cold. But when they came grumbling down to the kitchen, the little red hen was bright and busy and cheerful.

"Who will get some sticks to light the fire?" she
asked.

"I won't," said the cock.

"I won't," said the mouse.

"Then I will do it myself," said the little red hen.
So off she went and got the sticks.

"And now who will fill the kettle?" she asked.

"I won't," said the cock.

"I won't," said the mouse.

"Then I will do it myself," said the little red hen.
And she filled the kettle.

"And who will get the breakfast ready?" she asked as she put the kettle on to boil.

"I won't," said the cock.

"I won't," said the mouse.

"Then I will do it myself," said the little red hen.

At breakfast the cock upset the jug of milk, and the mouse scattered crumbs all over the floor, and they both quarreled and grumbled.

"Who will clear the table?" asked the little red hen.

"I won't," said the cock.

"I won't," said the mouse.

"Then I will do it myself," said the little red hen.

She cleared the table and mopped up the milk and swept away all the crumbs.

"And now who will help me make the beds?"
she asked.

"I won't," said the cock.

"I won't," said the mouse.

"Then I will do it myself," said the little red hen.

And she went upstairs while the lazy cock and
mouse sat down each in a comfortable chair by the
fire, where they soon fell fast asleep.

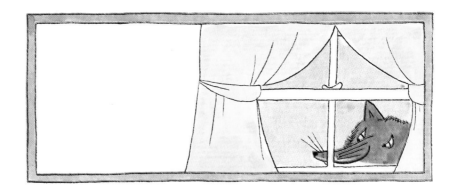

Now the big bad fox had crept up the hill and into the garden. If the cock and the mouse had not been sleeping, they would have seen his sharp eyes peering in at the window.

Knock, knock! went the fox at the door.

"Who could that be?" said the mouse, yawning.

"Go and see for yourself, if you want to know," said the cock.

"Perhaps it is the postman," said the mouse, "and perhaps he has a letter for me!" So without looking to see who it was, he turned the knob and opened the door.

As soon as he opened the door, in jumped the big bad fox.

"Eeek, eeek, eeek!" said the mouse as he tried to run up the chimney.

"Cock-a-doodle-doo!" crowed the cock as he jumped on the back of the biggest armchair.

But the fox only laughed and caught the little mouse by the tail and popped him into the sack, and he took the cock by the neck and popped him in, too.

Then the little red hen came running down the stairs to see what all the noise was about. So the fox caught her, too, and put her into the sack with the others.

Then he took a piece of string out of his pocket and tied up the mouth of the sack very tight indeed. After that, he threw the sack over his back, and off he set down the hill.

"Oh, I wish I hadn't been so cross," said the cock. "Oh, I wish I hadn't been so lazy," said the mouse. And the cock and the mouse began to cry.

"Don't be too sad," whispered the little red hen. "See, here is my little workbag, and in it there is a pair of scissors, and a thimble, and a needle and thread. Now, you wait and see what I am going to do. But be quiet!"

By then the sun was very hot, and the sack was
heavy, so the big bad fox thought he would lie down
under a tree and go to sleep for a while. As soon as
the fox began to snore, the little red hen took out
her scissors and snipped a hole in the sack just big
enough for the mouse to creep through.

"Quick!" she said to the mouse "Run as fast as you
can and bring back a stone as big as yourself."

And the mouse did.

"Push it in here," said the little red hen, and the
mouse pushed it into the sack.

Then the little red hen snipped away at the hole
until it was large enough for the cock to go through.

"Quick!" she said "Run as fast as you can and
bring back a stone as big as yourself."

Out flew the cock, and he soon came back with a
big stone which he too pushed into the sack.

Now the little red hen popped out and got a stone
as big as herself and pushed it into the sack. Then
she put on her thimble, took out her needle and
thread, and quickly sewed up the hole.

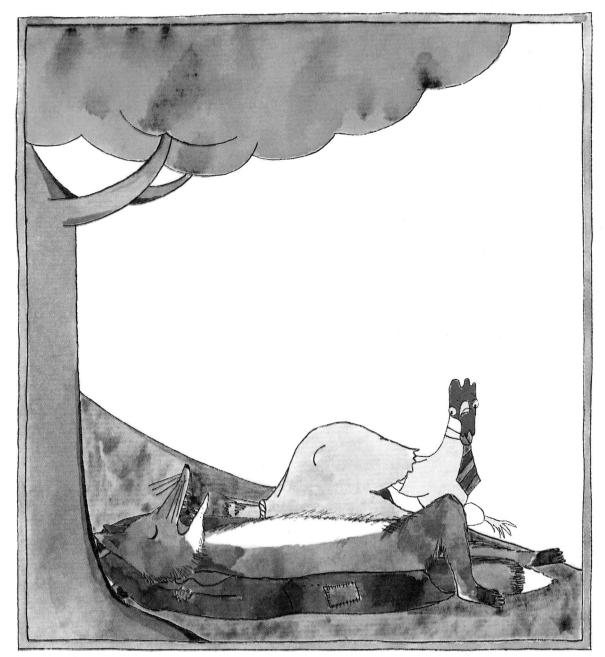

When the hole was sewed up, the cock and the mouse and the little red hen ran home very fast. They slammed the door and locked it tight. Not long after, the big bad fox woke up. He went grumbling and groaning down the hill, for the sack was very heavy.

When he came to the stream, *splash,* in went one foot, *splash,* in went the other, but the stones in the sack were so heavy that at the very next step down tumbled the big bad fox into a deep pool. And the four greedy little foxes had to go to bed without any supper.

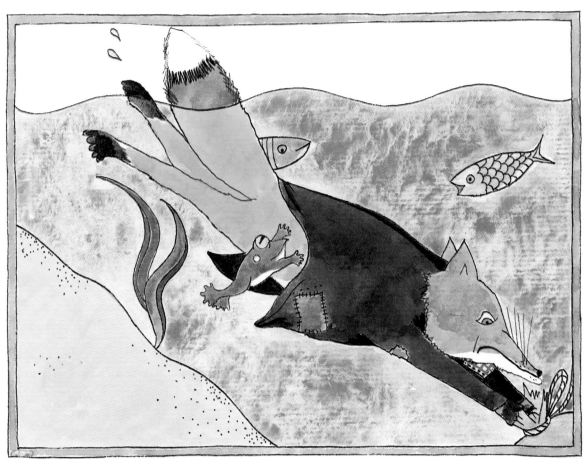

But the cock and the mouse never grumbled again. They lit the fire and filled the kettle, set the table, cooked the breakfast and made the beds, while the good little red hen had a holiday and sat resting in the big armchair in front of the fire.

No foxes ever troubled them again and they are still living happily in the pretty little house that stands on the hill.

The Gingerbread Man

Once upon a time there was a little old woman and a little old man, and they lived all alone. They were very happy together, but they wanted a child and since they had none, they decided to make one out of gingerbread. So one day the little old woman and the little old man made themselves a little gingerbread man, and they put him in the oven to bake.

When the gingerbread man was done, the little old woman opened the oven door and pulled out the pan. Out jumped the little gingerbread man—and away he ran. The little old woman and the little old man ran after him as fast as they could, but he just laughed and said, "Run, run, as fast as you can. You can't catch me! I'm the Gingerbread Man!"

And they couldn't catch him.

The gingerbread man ran on and on until he came to a cow.

"Stop, little gingerbread man," said the cow. "I want to eat you."

But the gingerbread man said, "I have run away from a little old woman and a little old man, and I can run away from you, too. I can, I can!"

And the cow began to chase the gingerbread man,
but the gingerbread man ran faster, and said, "Run,
run, as fast as you can. You can't catch me! I'm the
Gingerbread Man!"

And the cow couldn't catch him.

The gingerbread man ran on until he came to a horse.

"Please, stop, little gingerbread man," said the horse. "I want to eat you."

And the gingerbread man said, "I have run away from a little old woman, a little old man, and a cow, and I can run away from you, too. I can, I can!"

And the horse began to chase the gingerbread man, but the gingerbread man ran faster and called to the horse, "Run, run, as fast as you can. You can't catch me! I'm the Gingerbread Man!"

And the horse couldn't catch him.

By and by the gingerbread man came to a field full of farmers.

"Stop," said the farmers. "Don't run so fast. We want to eat you."

But the gingerbread man said, "I have run away from a little old woman, a little old man, a cow, and a horse, and I can run away from you, too. I can, I can!"

And the farmers began to chase him, but the gingerbread man ran faster than ever and said, "Run, run,
as fast as you can. You can't catch me! I'm the Gingerbread Man!"

And the farmers couldn't catch him.

The gingerbread man ran faster and faster. He ran
past a school full of children.

"Stop, little gingerbread man," said the children. "We want to eat you."

But the gingerbread man said, "I have run away from a little old woman, a little old man, a cow, and a horse, a field full of farmers, and I can run away from you, too. I can, I can!"

And the children began to chase him, but the gingerbread man ran faster as he said, "Run, run, as fast as you can. You can't catch me! I'm the Gingerbread Man!"

And the children couldn't catch him.

By this time the gingerbread man was so proud of himself he didn't think anyone could catch him. Pretty soon he saw a fox. The fox looked at him and began to run after him. But the gingerbread man said, "You can't catch me! I have run away from a little old woman, a little old man, a cow, a horse, a field full of farmers, a school full of children, and I can run away from you, too. I can, I can! Run, run, as fast as you can. You can't catch me! I'm the Gingerbread Man!"

"Oh," said the fox, "I do not want to catch you. I only want to help you run away."

Just then the gingerbread man came to a river. He could not swim across, and he had to keep running.

"Jump on my tail," said the fox. "I will take you across."

So the gingerbread man jumped on the fox's tail,

and the fox began to swim across the river. When he had gone a little way, he said to the gingerbread man, "You are too heavy on my tail. Jump on my back."

And the gingerbread man did.

The fox swam a little farther, and then he said, "I am afraid you will get wet on my back. Jump on my shoulder."

And the gingerbread man did.

In the middle of the river, the fox said, "Oh, dear, my shoulder is sinking. Jump on my nose, and I can hold you out of the water."

So the little gingerbread man jumped on the fox's nose, and the fox threw back his head and snapped his sharp teeth.

"Oh, dear," said the gingerbread man, "I am a quarter gone!"

Next minute he said, "Now I am half gone!"

And next minute he said, "Oh, my goodness gracious! I am three quarters gone!"

And then the gingerbread man never said anything more at all.

THE HOUSE THAT JACK BUILT

1. This is the house that Jack built.

2. This is the malt
   That lay in the house that Jack built.

3. This is the rat,
   That ate the malt
   That lay in the house that Jack built.

4. This is the cat,
   That killed the rat,
   That ate the malt
   That lay in the house that Jack built.

5. This is the dog,
   That worried the cat,
   That killed the rat,
   That ate the malt
   That lay in the house that Jack built.

6. This is the cow with the crumpled horn,
   That tossed the dog,
   That worried the cat,
   That killed the rat,
   That ate the malt
   That lay in the house that Jack built.

7. This is the maiden all forlorn,
   That milked the cow with the crumpled horn,
   That tossed the dog,
   That worried the cat,
   That killed the rat,
   That ate the malt
   That lay in the house that Jack built.

8. This is the man all tattered and torn,
   That kissed the maiden all forlorn,
   That milked the cow with the crumpled horn,
   That tossed the dog,
   That worried the cat,
   That killed the rat,
   That ate the malt
   That lay in the house that Jack built.

9. This is the priest all shaven and shorn,
   That married the man all tattered and torn,
   That kissed the maiden all forlorn,
   That milked the cow with the crumpled horn,
   That tossed the dog,
   That worried the cat,
   That killed the rat,
   That ate the malt
   That lay in the house that Jack built.

10. This is the cock that crowed in the morn,
That waked the priest all shaven and shorn,
That married the man all tattered and torn,
That kissed the maiden all forlorn,
That milked the cow with the crumpled horn,
That tossed the dog,
That worried the cat,
That killed the rat,
That ate the malt
That lay in the house that Jack built.

11. This is the farmer sowing his corn,
That kept the cock that crowed in the morn,
That waked the priest all shaven and shorn,
That married the man all tattered and torn,
That kissed the maiden all forlorn,
That milked the cow with the crumpled horn,
That tossed the dog,
That worried the cat,
That killed the rat,
That ate the malt
That lay in the house that Jack built.

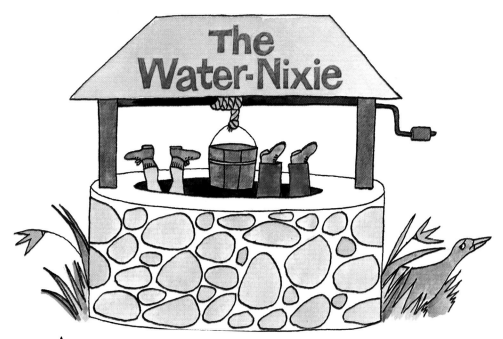

The Water-Nixie

A little brother and sister were once playing by a well, and they both fell in. Down below, there lived a water-nixie who said, "Now I have got you! You shall both work for me."

She gave the little girl a hank of dirty tangled flax to spin, and made her fetch water in a bucket that had a hole in it. The boy had to chop down a tree with a blunt ax, and they both got nothing to eat but dumplings, hard as stones.

One Sunday, when the nixie was at church, the children ran away. But as soon as church was over, the nixie followed them with long strides. The children saw her coming from far away, and the little girl quickly threw behind them her hairbrush, which turned into an immense hill of bristles with thousands and thousands of spikes. It was very difficult for the nixie to scramble across the spikes, but at last she got over, and began to run after them again. Then the boy threw down his comb which made a great ridge with a thousand times a thousand teeth, but the nixie managed to cross over that, too, and ran after them

again. Then the girl threw her mirror behind her. This turned into a great mountain made all of glass mirrors, and it was so slippery that the nixie could not climb it.

Then the nixie thought, "I will go home quickly and fetch my ax and chop that hill of glass mirrors in two!" But before she came back and chopped her way through, the children had run far away, and the nixie had to go home to her well again.

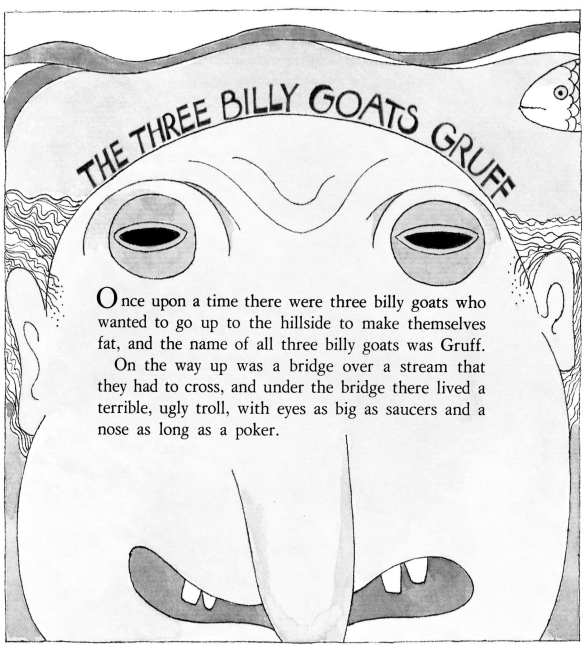

THE THREE BILLY GOATS GRUFF

Once upon a time there were three billy goats who wanted to go up to the hillside to make themselves fat, and the name of all three billy goats was Gruff.

On the way up was a bridge over a stream that they had to cross, and under the bridge there lived a terrible, ugly troll, with eyes as big as saucers and a nose as long as a poker.

First of all came the youngest billy goat Gruff to cross the bridge.

Trip, trap, trip, trap went the sound of his hooves on the bridge.

"Who's that tripping over the bridge?" roared the troll.

"Oh, it is only I, the tiniest billy goat Gruff. I'm going up to the hillside to make myself fat," said the billy goat, who had such a small voice.

"Now, I'm coming to gobble you up," said the troll.

"Oh, no, please don't eat me. I'm too little—that I am," said the billy goat. "Wait until the second billy goat Gruff comes. He's bigger. He'd make a much better dinner."

"Well, be off with you!" said the troll.

A little while later came the second billy goat Gruff to cross the bridge.

Trip, trap, trip, trap, trip, trap went the sound of his hooves on the bridge.

"Who's that tripping over the bridge?" roared the troll.

"Oh, it is I, the second billy goat Gruff, and I'm going up to the hillside to make myself fat," said the second billy goat Gruff, who hadn't such a small voice.

"Now, I'm coming to gobble you up," said the troll.

"Oh, no, please don't eat me. Wait until the big billy goat Gruff comes. He's bigger," said the second billy goat. "He'd make a much better dinner."

"Very well, be off with you," said the troll.

But just then up came the big billy goat Gruff.

Trip, trap, trip, trap, trip, trap, trip, trap! went the sound of his hooves on the bridge very loudly, for the big billy goat was so heavy that the bridge creaked and groaned under him.

"Who's that tramping over the bridge?" roared the troll.

"It is I, the big billy goat Gruff," said the big billy goat, who had a big hoarse voice of his own.

"Now, I'm coming to gobble you up!" roared the troll.

"Well come along! I've got two spears,
And I'll poke your eyeballs out at your ears.
I've got besides two great, big stones,
And I'll crush you to bits, both body and bones!"

That was what the big billy goat said. And that
was just what he did. And that was the last anyone

61

ever heard of the troll. Then the big billy goat went up to the hillside. There the three billy goats Gruff got so fat they were scarcely able to walk home. And if the fat hasn't fallen off them, why they're still fat, and so,

> Snip, snap, snout,
> This tale's told out.

Henny-Penny was pecking at grain in the barnyard when suddenly something hit her on the head.

"Oh, my goodness!" said Henny-Penny. "The sky is falling. I must go and tell the king."

So she went along and she went along until she met Cocky-Locky.

"Where are you going?" asked Cocky-Locky.

"Oh, I'm going to tell the king the sky is falling," said Henny-Penny.

"May I come with you?" asked Cocky-Locky.

"Yes, you may," said Henny-Penny. So Henny-Penny and Cocky-Locky went to tell the king the sky was falling.

They went along and they went along until they
met Ducky-Daddles.

"Where are you going?" asked Ducky-Daddles.

"Oh, we're going to tell the king the sky is falling,"
said Henny-Penny and Cocky-Locky.

"May I come with you?" asked Ducky-Daddles.

"Yes, you may," said Henny-Penny and Cocky-Locky. So Henny-Penny, Cocky-Locky, and Ducky-Daddles went to tell the king the sky was falling.

They went along and they went along until they met Goosey-Poosey.

"Where are you going?" asked Goosey-Poosey.

"Oh, we're going to tell the king the sky is falling," said Henny-Penny, Cocky-Locky, and Ducky-Daddles.

"May I come with you?" asked Goosey-Poosey.

"Yes, you may," said Henny-Penny, Cocky-Locky, and Ducky-Daddles. So Henny-Penny, Cocky-Locky, Ducky-Daddles, and Goosey-Poosey went to tell the king the sky was falling.

They went along and they went along until they met Turkey-Lurkey.

"Where are you going?" asked Turkey-Lurkey.

"Oh, we're going to tell the king the sky is falling," said Henny-Penny, Cocky-Locky, Ducky-Daddles, and Goosey-Poosey.

"May I come with you?" asked Turkey-Lurkey.

"Yes, you may," said Henny-Penny, Cocky-Locky, Ducky-Daddles, and Goosey-Poosey. So Henny-Penny, Cocky-Locky, Ducky-Daddles, Goosey-Poosey, and Turkey-Lurkey went to tell the king the sky was falling.

They went along and they went along until they met Foxy-Woxy, and Foxy-Woxy asked Henny-Penny, Cocky-Locky, Ducky-Daddles, Goosey-Poosey, and Turkey-Lurkey, "Where are you going?"

And Henny-Penny, Cocky-Locky, Ducky-Daddles, Goosey-Poosey, and Turkey-Lurkey said, "Oh, we're going to tell the king the sky is falling."

"But this is not the right way to go to the king," said Foxy-Woxy. "I know the right way. Do you want to follow me?"

"Oh, yes, Foxy-Woxy," said Henny-Penny, Cocky-Locky, Ducky-Daddles, Goosey-Poosey, and Turkey-Lurkey. So Foxy-Woxy, Henny-Penny, Cocky-Locky, Ducky-Daddles, Goosey-Poosey, and Turkey-Lurkey all went to tell the king the sky was falling.

They went along and they went along until they
came to a dark hole. Now this was the door of Foxy-
Woxy's cave. But Foxy-Woxy said to Henny-Penny,
Cocky-Locky, Ducky-Daddles, Goosey-Poosey, and
Turkey-Lurkey, "This is the right way to go to the
king. You will get there quickly if you follow me."

"Oh, yes, indeed!" said Henny-Penny, Cocky-Locky,
Ducky-Daddles, Goosey-Poosey, and Turkey-Lurkey.

Foxy-Woxy went into his cave and waited for Henny-Penny, Cocky-Locky, Ducky-Daddles, Goosey-Poosey, and Turkey-Lurkey to follow him.

Turkey-Lurkey went through the dark hole first. He hadn't gone far when Foxy-Woxy ate up Turkey-Lurkey. Then Goosey-Poosey went in, and Foxy-Woxy ate up Goosey-Poosey. Then Ducky-Daddles went in, and Foxy-Woxy ate up Ducky-Daddles. Then Cocky-Locky went in, but before Foxy-Woxy could eat him up, Cocky-Locky crowed, "Cock-a-doodle-do!"

As soon as Henny-Penny heard Cocky-Locky crow, "Cock-a-doodle-do!" she said, "Oh, my goodness! It is time to lay my egg!"

And she ran home to the barnyard and never did get to tell the king the sky was falling.

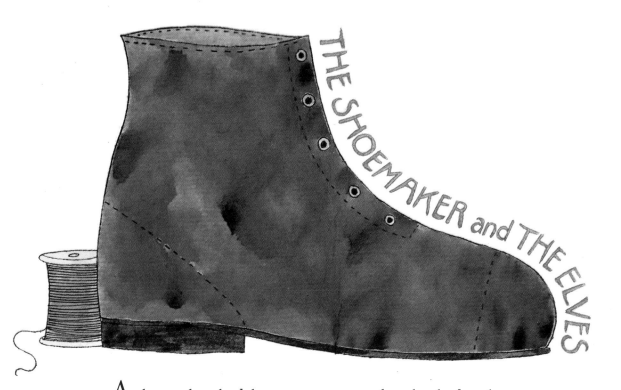

THE SHOEMAKER and THE ELVES

A shoemaker had become so poor that he had only
enough leather for one pair of shoes. In the evening
he cut out the leather for the shoes he would make
next morning, and then he went to bed. But in the
morning, when he was about to go to work, the pair
of shoes stood all finished on his cobbler's bench.
When he saw them, the shoemaker was very surprised,
and did not know what to think. And when he looked
closely at the shoes, he saw there was not one bad
stitch in them; they were perfect in every way.

Before long, a customer came into his shop and bought the shoes. But because they were so beautiful and so well made the customer paid extra for them, and the shoemaker was able to buy leather for two pairs of shoes.

He cut them out at night, and woke up early to sew the shoes together, but once again, there was no need to do so. For when he got up, the shoes were already made. Customers came, too, and he made enough money that day to buy leather for four pairs of shoes. Again next morning he found the four pairs of shoes made, and so it went on—what leather he cut in the evening was finished by morning, and the shoes were always perfect and well made, so the shoemaker became a rich man.

One winter evening, when the man had finished cutting out the leather, he said to his wife, "What if we were to stay up tonight and see who it is that helps us so?"

His wife liked that idea, and so the two of them hid themselves in a corner of the shop, and waited and watched.

When it was exactly midnight, two little naked elves came. They sat down promptly on the cobbler's bench, took the cutout leather, and began to stitch and began to sew and began to hammer. And all this they did so nimbly and so well that the shoemaker could not turn his eyes away for amazement. The two little elves did not stop working until the shoes were all done. Then quickly and quietly they ran away.

Next morning the woman said, "Those little elves have made us rich, and we should show them that we are grateful for it. They run about so without any clothes on. They must be cold. I will make them each a little hat and shirt and vest and trousers, and I will knit them each a pair of stockings. And you can make two little pairs of shoes."

"I will be happy to," said the shoemaker.

A few nights later they laid their presents on the cobbler's bench in place of the cutout leather and hid themselves where they could watch the two little elves.

At midnight the little elves came bounding in, ready to go to work at once. They were very surprised to find no cutout leather, only the pretty little clothes. They touched the little vests and hats and shirts and trousers, the striped stockings and leather shoes. Suddenly they smiled with delight when they realized the clothes were theirs. They dressed themselves quickly and sang:

"We are boys so fine to see,
Why should we now cobblers be?"

Then they danced and skipped off the cobbler's bench and around the shop and out the door. From then on they came no more, but the shoemaker and his wife lived happily and well.

Teeny-Tiny

There was once a teeny-tiny woman who lived in a teeny-tiny house in a teeny-tiny town. One day this teeny-tiny woman put on her teeny-tiny hat and went out of her teeny-tiny house to take a teeny-tiny walk. When the teeny-tiny woman had gone a teeny-tiny way, she came to a teeny-tiny gate. Then the teeny-tiny woman opened the teeny-tiny gate and went into a teeny-tiny churchyard. In the teeny-tiny churchyard she saw a teeny-tiny bone upon a teeny-tiny grave, and the teeny-tiny woman said, "This teeny-tiny bone will make some teeny-tiny soup for my teeny-tiny supper." And the teeny-tiny woman took the teeny-tiny bone from the teeny-tiny grave and put it in her teeny-tiny pocket and went back to her teeny-tiny house.

When the teeny-tiny woman got inside her teeny-tiny house, she was a teeny-tiny bit sleepy, so she put the teeny-tiny bone into her teeny-tiny cupboard, and then she went up her teeny-tiny stairs and climbed into her teeny-tiny bed.

After the teeny-tiny woman had closed her teeny-tiny eyes for a teeny-tiny nap, she was awakened by a teeny-tiny voice from the teeny-tiny cupboard down the teeny-tiny stairs that said:

"Give me my bone!"

When she heard this the teeny-tiny woman was a teeny-tiny bit frightened, so she hid her teeny-tiny head under her teeny-tiny blanket and went to sleep again. And when she had slept a teeny-tiny time, the teeny-tiny voice cried out again a teeny-tiny bit louder:

"Give me my bone!"

This made the teeny-tiny woman a teeny-tiny bit more frightened, so she hid her teeny-tiny head a teeny-tiny bit farther under the teeny-tiny blanket. And when the teeny-tiny woman had gone to sleep again for a teeny-tiny time, the teeny-tiny voice from the teeny-tiny cupboard down the teeny-tiny stairs said a teeny-tiny bit louder:

"Give me my bone!"

By now the teeny-tiny woman was a teeny-tiny bit more frightened, but she lifted up her teeny-tiny head from under her teeny-tiny blanket and said in her loudest teeny-tiny voice:

"TAKE IT!"

THE THREE LITTLE PIGS

Once upon a time there was an old sow with three little pigs, and she sent them out into the world to seek their fortune.

The first little pig met a man with a bundle of straw and said to him, "Please, man, give me that straw to build a house." And the man did, and the little pig built a house with the straw.

Along came a wolf who knocked at the door and said, "Little pig, little pig, let me come in."

And the little pig answered, "No, no, by the hair of my chinny, chin, chin!"

So the wolf said, "Then I'll huff and I'll puff and I'll blow your house in!"

So the wolf huffed and he puffed and he blew the house in and ate up the little pig.

The second little pig met a man with a bundle of sticks and said to him, "Please, man, give me those sticks to build a house." And the man did, and the little pig built a house with the sticks.

Then along came the wolf who knocked at the door and said, "Little pig, little pig, let me come in."

And the little pig answered, "No, no, by the hair of my chinny, chin, chin!"

So the wolf said, "Then I'll huff and I'll puff and I'll blow your house in!"

So the wolf huffed and he puffed, and he puffed and he huffed, and he blew the house down and ate up the little pig.

The third little pig met a man with a load of bricks and said to him, "Please, man, give me those bricks to build a house." And the man gave him the bricks, and the little pig built a house with them.

Then the wolf came, just as he had to the other little pigs, and knocked on the door and said, "Little pig, little pig, let me come in."

And the little pig answered, "No, no, by the hair of my chinny, chin, chin!"

So the wolf said, "Then I'll huff and I'll puff and I'll blow your house in!"

Well, the wolf huffed and puffed, and he puffed and he huffed, and he huffed and he puffed, but he could not blow that house down. So when he found that he could **not**, he said, "Little pig, I know where there are some nice turnips."

"Where?" said the little pig.

"Down in Farmer Smith's field," said the wolf. "If you will be ready tomorrow morning at six o'clock I will come and get you, and we can go together to pick some turnips for dinner."

"Very well," said the little pig, and the wolf went away.

The next morning the little pig got up at five o'clock and picked the turnips and got back home before the wolf came to get him at six.

When the wolf arrived, he said, "Little pig, are you ready?"

The little pig said, "I have been there and back, and I have a nice potful of turnips for dinner."

The wolf felt very angry at this, but he said in his nicest voice, "Little pig, I know where there is a fine apple tree."

"Where?" said the little pig.

"Over in Mary's garden," said the wolf. "And if you will not trick me, I will come for you tomorrow morning at five o'clock, and we will pick some apples."

Well, the little pig got up next morning at four o'clock and went off for the apples, hoping to get home before the wolf came for him. But he had farther to go this time, and he had to climb the tree besides, so just as he was climbing down the tree, he saw the wolf coming, and this frightened the little pig very much.

The wolf stood under the tree and said, "Why, little pig! Are you here before me? Are they nice apples?"

"Oh, yes," said the little pig, "they are good and sweet. Here, I will throw one down to you."

And he threw the apple so far that while the wolf was running off to get it, the little pig jumped down from the tree and ran all the way home.

Next day the wolf came again, and said to the little pig, "Little pig, there is a fair in town this afternoon. Will you go with me?"

"Oh, yes," said the little pig, "I will. What time will you come to get me?"

"I will come at three," said the wolf.

So the little pig left early, as usual, and bought a butter churn at the fair. He was walking home with it when he saw the wolf coming. The little pig did not know what to do. So he got inside the butter churn to hide. While he was squeezing himself in, he turned the butter churn around on its side, and it rolled down the hill with the little pig inside. And it rolled right down the hill toward the wolf, and the wolf was so frightened that he ran home without ever going to the fair.

Later he went to the little pig's house and told him about the big scary thing that had come rolling down the hill to chase him.

Then the little pig said, "Ha! So I scared you, did I? That was only the butter churn I bought at the fair, and I was inside."

When he heard this the wolf was very, very angry indeed, and he declared that he would eat up that little pig, and he was coming down the chimney to get him.

As soon as the little pig heard this, he filled up a large pot with water and built up a blazing fire. Just as the wolf was coming down the chimney the little pig took the lid off the pot, and in fell the wolf.

The little pig popped the lid back on the pot, boiled up the wolf, ate him for supper, and lived happily ever after.

LAZY JACK

Once upon a time there was a boy whose name was Jack, and he lived with his mother in a little house. They were very poor. Jack's mother earned her living by spinning, but Jack was so lazy he would do nothing but sit in the sun in the summer and sit by the fire in the winter. And as he always sat and sat and did nothing useful, everyone called him Lazy Jack. At last his mother told him one Monday morning that if he did not begin to work for his food, she would turn him out of the house to feed himself as best he could.

So Jack went out and went to work next day for a neighbor who paid him a penny. But on his way home Jack lost his penny.

"You stupid boy," said his mother, "you should have put it in your pocket."

"I'll do that next time," said Jack.

Well, the next day Jack went out again and went to work for a milkman who gave him a little bucket of milk for his day's work. Jack took the bucket and put it into his pocket. It splashed around as he walked, and it was all gone before he got home.

"Dear me!" said Jack's mother when she saw his wet jacket and the good milk all gone. "You should have carried it on your head."

"I'll do that next time," said Jack.

The next day Jack went to work for a grocer who gave him a soft cheese for his day's work. In the evening Jack took the cheese and went home with it on his head. By the time he got home the cheese had melted. Part of it was lost, and part matted into Jack's hair.

"You silly," said Jack's mother, "you should have carried it carefully in your hands."

"I'll do that next time," said Jack.

Now the next day Jack went out and went to work for a baker who would not give him anything for his day's work but a large tomcat. Jack took the cat and began carrying it very carefully in his hands. But before long the cat had scratched him so badly that he had to let it go.

When he got home, his mother said to him, "You poor fool, you should have tied it with a string and pulled it along after you."

"I'll do that next time," said Jack.

The next day Jack went to work for a butcher who paid him with a piece of beef. Jack took the beef, tied it to a string, and pulled it after him. He pulled it in the dirt, so that by the time he got home the meat was not fit to eat. His mother was especially angry with him this time, for the next day was Sunday, and they would have to have cabbage for their dinner.

"You ninny," Jack's mother said to her son, "you should have carried it on your shoulder."

"I'll do that next time," said Jack.

Well, when Monday came, Lazy Jack went out once more and went to work for a farmer, who gave him a donkey for his trouble. Although Jack was strong, he found it hard to hoist the donkey onto his shoulders, but at last he did it and began walking slowly home.

Along the road he passed a house where a rich man lived with his only daughter, a very beautiful girl. But this beautiful girl had never laughed in her life, not once. So her father had said that any man who made her laugh would be her husband. Now the beautiful girl just happened to be looking out the window when Jack came by with the donkey on his shoulders. The poor beast had its legs sticking up in the air, and it was kicking and heehawing with all its might. The sight was so funny she burst out laughing, and she laughed and laughed and laughed some more. Her father was overjoyed and he kept his promise by marrying her to Lazy Jack. So Jack became a rich gentleman and never had to do another day's work. He and his wife lived in a large house very happily, and Jack's mother came and lived there, too.

One day a dog stole a big soup bone from a butcher shop and ran off with it. He ran and he ran, out of the town and down the road, and onto a bridge that crossed a bright clear river. Suddenly the dog saw his own reflection in the water. He stopped.

"Who is that dog with that nice big bone?" he thought to himself and growled. "I want that bone, too! It looks bigger and better than mine," he thought and growled a little louder. He snarled, and the dog he saw in the water snarled, too.

Then the dog opened his mouth and made a grab for the other dog's bone. But as soon as he opened his mouth, the bone fell into the river, and the dog had nothing to eat that day. No, nothing at all.

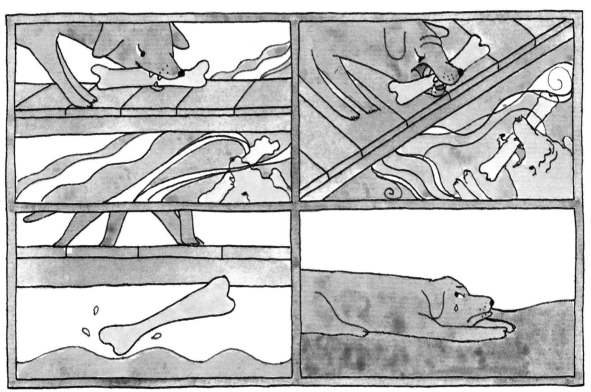

Once upon a time there was a dear little girl whose grandmother made her a beautiful cape and hood of red velvet. She wore it wherever she went, and so everyone called her "Little Red Riding Hood."

One day her mother said to her, "Little Red Riding Hood, here is a piece of cake and some good soup. Take them straight to your grandmother and go quickly, for she is sick in bed."

The grandmother lived in the forest, half a mile from the village. Just as Little Red Riding Hood entered the forest, she met a wolf. Little Red Riding Hood did not know how wicked the wolf was, and she was not afraid of him.

"Good morning, Little Red Riding Hood. Where are you going this fine day?" said the wolf.

"I am going to Grandmother's to take her some cake and some good soup," said Little Red Riding Hood.

"Where does your grandmother live?" asked the wolf.

"She lives in a little house under three large oak trees. There is a berry-bush hedge. Surely you must know it," said Little Red Riding Hood.

And the wicked wolf thought, "What a sweet little girl! She would certainly be good to eat. And if I am clever, I will be able to eat her up and the old woman, too."

So he walked pleasantly along the path with Little Red Riding Hood, and he said, "Why are you so serious, Little Red Riding Hood? Look at those pretty flowers growing over there. Listen to those birds singing. Why don't you stop and play? Surely your grandmother can wait until lunchtime for her cake and soup."

Little Red Riding Hood looked at the flowers growing in the sunlight beneath the trees, and she thought, "I will pick Grandmother a bouquet," and she ran off the path and into the forest, picking flowers as she ran. And as soon as she had picked one, she saw another that was prettier still, and so she went deeper and deeper into the forest.

Meanwhile the wolf ran straight to the grandmother's house and gulped the old woman down.
Then he put on her nightgown and cap, and got into
her bed, and pulled up the covers.

At last, when Little Red Riding Hood had picked
as many flowers as she could carry, she returned to
the path and set out again for her grandmother's
house.

When she got there, she saw her grandmother in
bed with the blankets pulled up high and thought
she looked very strange.

"Oh, Grandmother," she said, "what big ears you
have!"

"The better to hear you with, my dear" was the
reply.

"But, Grandmother, what big eyes you have!"

"The better to see you with, my dear."

"But, Grandmother, what big teeth you have!"
"The better to eat you with!" said the wolf, and
jumped out of bed and gulped down Little Red Riding
Hood.

Then the wolf climbed back into bed and fell asleep. He soon began to snore very loudly. A friendly woodchopper was passing by the house, and he thought, "Listen to the old woman snore! I will stop in and see if she needs anything today."

And the wood chopper went into the house and saw the wolf sleeping and snoring in the grandmother's bed.

Quickly and quietly the woodchopper took out his sharp knife and carefully, he cut a hole in the stomach of the wolf. He saw some red velvet shining there, so he made the hole a bit bigger, and out jumped Little Red Riding Hood, crying, "Ah, how frightened I have been! How dark it was inside the wolf!"

And then the woodchopper made the hole another bit bigger, and out came the grandmother, alive but very weak indeed.

But the grandmother ate the cake and drank the good soup and felt much better. And Little Red Riding Hood went home through the forest, and no harm came to her.

The Little Pot

There was once a poor but good little girl who lived alone with her mother, and they no longer had anything to eat. The little girl went into the forest, and there she met an old woman who felt sorry for her. So the old woman gave her a little pot which when she said, "Cook, little pot, cook," would cook good sweet porridge. And when she said, "Stop, little pot," it would stop cooking. The child took the pot home to her mother, and now they were no longer hungry, for they ate sweet porridge as often as they wished.

One day the little girl had gone out, and her mother said, "Cook, little pot, cook." And the pot did cook, and she ate until she was full. Then she wanted the pot to stop cooking, but she did not know the right words to say to make it stop. Only the little girl knew that, and she was not at home. So the pot went on cooking, and porridge bubbled over the edge,

and still it cooked on until the kitchen and the whole house were full of porridge, and then the next house, and then the whole street. And everyone in town wanted the pot to stop cooking, but no one knew how to stop it.

At last, when only one single house remained that was not covered with porridge, the little girl came home. She said, "Stop, little pot," and it stopped cooking. And whoever wanted to return to town had to eat his way back.

The Star Money

There was once upon a time a good, kind little girl who had no mother and no father and who was so poor she had no house to live in and no bed to sleep in. She was so poor she had nothing, but the clothes she wore and a little piece of bread in her pocket. All alone she went out into the world.

She had not gone far before she met an old man who said, "Ah, give me something to eat. I am so hungry."

And the little girl gave him her piece of bread and went on again. But before long, she met a little child who moaned and said, "My head is cold. Give me something to cover it with."

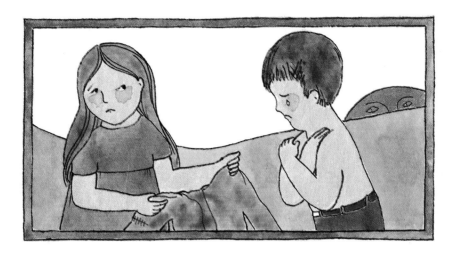

So she gave him her hat, and when she had walked a little farther, she met another child who had no jacket, and he too was cold. So she gave him her own, and a little farther on, a child begged for a dress, and she gave that away also. Then she came to a forest, and it was dark.

Soon she met another child who cried and shivered
and said, "I am so cold!" And the little girl thought,
"It is dark and no one can see me anyway." And so
she gave away all the clothes she had.

And as she stood, with not one single thing left, suddenly some stars fell down at her feet. And when she looked, she saw they were not stars at all but shiny gold and silver pieces of money. And although she had just given all her clothes away, she found she was dressed in new ones, much better and warmer than the old. So she put the money in her pocket. Never again was she cold or hungry, and she was happy all the days of her life.